the old one

D0380566

This book belongs to:

Mack

THE TRAPPS FAMILY ADVENTURES

the old one

By LAWRENCE E.R. ADAMS

Illustrations by ROBERT G. ADAMS

TRAPPS PUBLISHING

Copyright © by Lawrence E.R. Adams and Robert G. Adams

First Printed in 2007
Printed in Canada

All Rights Reserved. No part of this work covered by the copyright hereon may be reproduced in any form or by any means — graphic, electronic or mechanical — without prior written permission of the publisher, except for reviewers who may quote brief passages. Any request for photocopying, recording, taping or storage in an information retrieval system of any part of this book shall be directed in writing to the publisher.

THE PUBLISHER:
Trapps Publishing
P.O. Box 212
Irricana, Alberta, Canada T0M 1B0

Library and Archives Canada Cataloguing in Publication

Adams, Lawrence E.R. (Lawrence Edward Roy), 1941 –
The Old One / by Lawrence E.R. Adams ; illustrations by Robert G. Adams.

(TRAPPS family adventures)
Includes index.
ISBN 978-0-9781532-0-5

1.   Inuit—Canada—Fiction. 2. Inuit mythology—Fiction. I.
         Title. II. Series.

PS8601.D454043 2007 C813'.6 C2007-904350-X

Cover: Robert G. Adams
Printing: Friesens Corporation

For my son Robert

He inspired me to write this first novel. Without his help these books would never have been written.

DISCLAIMER

All the characters in this book are fictitious, any similarity between any living or deceased person is merely a coincidence.

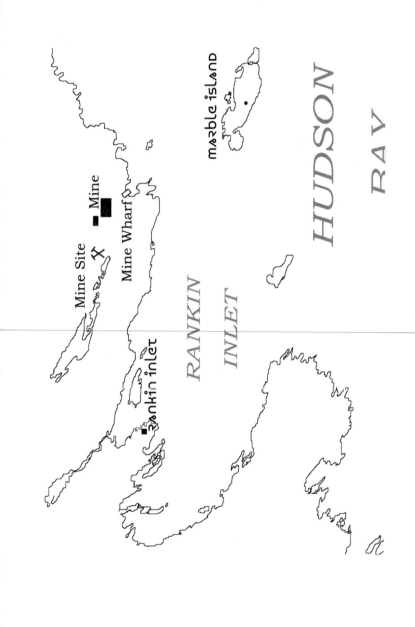

Mine

Mine Site

Mine Wharf

Rankin Inlet

RANKIN

INLET

HUDSON

BAY

marble island

CONTENTS

PROLOGUE

It wasn't the call of the North that brought the Trapps family to the vast treeless region of Canada's North, known as the Tundra. This trip had nothing to do with the romance that "the call of the North" evoked; this wasn't even going to be a holiday. Numerous hours of backbreaking work would dominate the expedition, or so they thought.

Max Trapps, a world-class archaeologist, has led expeditions to numerous places in the world conducting excavations to uncover the secrets of the past. He has been chosen to conduct an archaeological dig at an ancient Inuit settlement. Workers at the Blue Diamond Mine, approximately thirty kilometres northeast of Rankin Inlet on the west shore of the Hudson Bay in the Northwest Territories, made the discovery while working near their airstrip. For the duration of the dig, the mining company is generously supplying the food and lodgings for the entire Trapps Family.

When Amy and her brothers, Ty and Parker, meet "THE OLD ONE," the secrets and mysteries of the North and the Inuit way of life will be laid bare before them. Nothing the kids might have done before they left their home in Calgary could have prepared them for the adventures they are about to experience. They are entering an environment that few people have ever seen and fewer will ever live in. It is a harsh and unforgiving land that holds untold beauty, mystery, and adventure for those who dare to accept its challenges. The North is home for the Inuit, the only race of humans who are able to live under its conditions without assistance from the outside world. The Inuit's ability to adapt to their environment allows them to reap the bounty of the North. Only the most adventurous and well-equipped explorers have been able to penetrate the Inuit's habitat and live to tell about it.

Amy's curiosity and her thirst for knowledge sometimes gets her into jams that requires the help of her brothers to get out of. She enjoys assisting her father during excavations and likes nothing better than discovering a relic from the past and unlocking its secrets. Ty is twelve, one year younger than Amy, and a gifted athlete. His favorite sport is hockey and if he were allowed, he would play it twenty-four hours a day. Parker, who is one year younger than Ty, doesn't possess his brother's athletic abilities, but his determination to succeed and to not be outdone by anyone makes him a worthy opponent. He possesses a photographic memory, which has proven to be an asset when his sister gets them involved in one of her many schemes.

chapter 1

the chair

Sunday, September 15, 1985

Dear Diary,

My family has embarked on the most exciting adventure to Canada's far North. Mr. Munro gave us something to look forward to when he told us the story about The Old One, who had his own chair in the kitchen.

Amy

*   *   *

One particular chair in the camp kitchen, where all the meals are taken, is of great interest to the young Trapps. Since their arrival five days ago, they have been checking to see who would occupy THE CHAIR.

Bob Munro, the mine superintendent and their host, had advised them that this chair, closest to the serving counter leaning against the table, is reserved for THE OLD ONE.

"Who is THE OLD ONE?" Amy asked.

"You'll know when you see him, I doubt you've ever seen anyone like him before," replied Mr. Munro.

"Is he one of the owners?" Ty asked as he looked at Mr. Munro.

"No, he's actually an old Inuit, he just comes and goes as he pleases. Let me tell you something about THE OLD ONE. One night last year when my wife, Gwen, and I came for supper, it began to snow and the wind started to blow. By the time we finished supper you couldn't see your hand in front of your face. We thought the storm would blow over but it didn't; it just blew harder. Before we realized what was happening, we were in a full-blown Arctic blizzard. Three days later, we were still stuck in the kitchen weathering the storm," explained Mr. Munro.

"How come you didn't go to your house?" inquired Amy, as she stared at Mr. Munro.

"When a blizzard strikes up here, you stay where you are. Under no circumstances do you ever leave a building during a blizzard. I can tell you with a great deal of sincerity there's nothing that will make you wish you were somewhere else more than a howling Arctic blizzard." Mr. Munro paused to let the group appreciate the dire warning about leaving a building during a blizzard. "As I was saying, about three o'clock in the afternoon of the third day, the kitchen door opened and in walked THE OLD ONE, accompanied by the howling wind and blowing snow. He shook the snow off himself and sat down in that very chair." Mr. Munro pointed to the chair leaning against the table. "You should have seen the Inuit cooks; they just fell over themselves getting cookies and hot tea for THE OLD ONE. Gwen and I were just dumbfounded. We couldn't believe anyone would be out in a storm like that! After he finished eating and drinking he got up and just walked out the door into that raging blizzard. I thought for sure I would never see him alive again! But about a week after the storm ended, there he was: as big as life, out near the pit! Right then I said to myself, there is something about that old man that I will never understand, and as long as I'm the boss, that

15

chair will be reserved for him."

"Does he work here?" asked Amy.

"No, he doesn't. When we started to build the mine three years ago, he would come out and watch the work being done. When I think back now it seems that he would just appear, one minute he would be there and the next he would be gone. I can't recall ever seeing him coming or going," said Mr. Munro, a bewildered look on his face.

"Wow Jiminy-Willie-Peppers, you mean like magic?" Parker blurted out, his eyes growing larger.

"That's quite a saying, Jiminy what?" asked Mr. Munro.

"Oh, don't mind him Mr. Munro, he always says that when he's excited," explained Amy.

"Oh okay, well, I don't know. I wouldn't go so far as to say it's magic, it just seems that one minute he's there and the next he's not. I had asked if he was looking for a job, but the other Inuit miners said he didn't need a job; he lives by the old ways, off the land hunting and fishing. They told me he was just curious about the mine and wanted to see what was happening. One of the miners told me he doesn't speak English; they

16

just call him THE OLD ONE. If he wants something he always lets us know through one of the Inuit fellows or by his actions," Mr. Munro said.

"He must have a name!" Ty said to Mr. Munro.

"Yes, he probably does, but everyone refers to him as THE OLD ONE, and that's the only name I know him by. You'll see him, don't worry; he'll be along one of these days. When you do see him I doubt you'll ever forget him, he leaves a lasting impression," replied Mr. Munro as he shrugged his shoulders and smiled at the kids.

The kids' minds were running wild, trying to imagine who would be so important as to have his own reserved chair in the kitchen. Even Mr. Munro didn't have his own chair!

The kids checked the kitchen at every opportunity; they didn't want to miss seeing THE OLD ONE. Their curiosity had been aroused. After all, Mr. Munro had said he seemed to appear and disappear at will. Amy was almost beside herself with the anticipation of meeting the mystery man.

After five days of checking the kitchen, the kids were starting to think they would never see THE OLD ONE. Amy kept up the watch

17

religiously and continued to visit the kitchen wherever she could. Ty and Parker got lost in their new surroundings and spent most of their time exploring their new environment.

chapter ii

the old one

Saturday, September 21, 1985

Dear Diary,
    I had almost given up hope of ever seeing THE OLD ONE. When Mr. Munro told us about the old Inuit man called THE OLD ONE, he didn't realize he was opening a world to us we never knew existed.
    Amy

*   *   *

The morning of their sixth day, Amy was busy assisting her father at the dig, while Ty and

Parker kept themselves occupied by helping get the outdoor rink ready for its first layer of ice. Now that the weather was getting colder, they were hoping to get the ice in and start playing hockey. They'd already received the first snowfall of the year and could feel a nip in the air; winter would not be far behind. After working all morning at the dig Amy returned to the kitchen for lunch. When lunch was finished she stayed home to help her mother.

With her chores completed by about three o'clock in the afternoon, Amy called her brothers and they went to the kitchen for cocoa. The interior of a warm building would be a welcome relief from the bitter cold wind that was blowing.

As the kids approached the kitchen they could hear the Inuit ladies talking excitedly. When they entered, the ladies were grouped around THE CHAIR, fussing over the occupant.

The kids stopped in their tracks. They realized they were now staring at THE OLD ONE!

There was nothing that could have prepared the kids for what they were seeing now. They stood with their mouths open and stared at the old man who occupied THE CHAIR. The gray hair that hung to his shoulders had long ago replaced his shiny black hair. His face resembled the road map of time, as if each crease had a story to tell about its journey through life. Where he sat he looked to be small in stature probably no more than five feet tall, with broad shoulders. While appearing small there was no mistaking the strength that emanated from his very being. This was not a man anyone would trifle with, his every movement demanded respect. The kids had never seen anyone so attired. THE OLD ONE was wearing a caribou parka with polar bear pants and sealskin mukluks; he was a sight from the past rarely seen today.

Cradling a tin cup in his gnarled old hands, he gingerly sipped piping hot tea and ate cookies the cooks placed in front of him. All the while, the ladies hung on his every word, and made a great to-do over him. It was quite apparent that he enjoyed the attention he was receiving.

* * *

"Well come in and sit down, don't stand there staring, haven't you seen an old man before?" said a voice.

The voice jolted the kids back to reality and they looked around to see who had spoken. They were alone, no one was near them!

"Get your cocoa and sit down, that's what you came for isn't it?" the voice asked.

Although she spoke not a word, Amy felt herself saying, *"who are you and where are you?"*

Something awoke in the kids they did not know existed. They now have the ability to communicate through their Inuas, the spiritual occupant or spirit helpers that reside in all living and inanimate things.

"I am Kadluk, the one they call THE OLD ONE, and you have been waiting for me to come, haven't you?" asked the voice.

The kids realized the voice was coming from THE OLD ONE who occupied THE CHAIR.

"How did you know we were waiting for you to come? Mr. Munro told us that you don't speak English, so how is it that you are talking to my brothers and me? How can we be communicating when we don't speak the same language?" Amy asked.

"Sila told me there were some young Kabloonas at the mine who showed interest in the old ways. I am conversing with you through our Inuas," said Kadluk.

"You mean we can talk to each other and no one

knows we're talking and who is Sila and what are Kabloonas and Inuas?" cried Amy.

"Yeah that's what I'd like to know!" exclaimed Ty.

"Jiminy-Willie-Peppers, this is starting to get creepy," yelled Parker, as he frantically looked around.

"Yes, you have the ability to speak to each other and talk to the spirits as I do, for you possess the traits that a shaman must possess. Sila is the all-pervasive spirit that resides in the air. Kabloona is the Inuit word for white man. Inuas are the spiritual occupants or spirit helpers, who reside in all living and inanimate objects," Kadluk replied.

"How come Mr. Munro says you don't speak English? You're speaking English to us, why don't you talk to him?" asked Amy.

"No, I don't speak English, I only know Inuktitut, but we can communicate through our Inuas. I don't speak to Mr. Munro because he does not possess the abilities of a shaman as you and I do. We could talk to his Inua, but he would not know we were conversing," replied Kadluk.

"This is scary, you're way over there and not even looking at us, let alone talking to us. In fact, you're talking to the Inuit ladies. How can you do that?" questioned Parker.

"Don't be alarmed, our Inuas are conversing. Sila said you might be uneasy at first but you would overcome your doubts. Your thirst for adventure and knowledge is far stronger than any fears you may have. Is that not so?" asked Kadluk with an inquiring tone to his voice.

"Yes, we love to explore and have new adventures," shouted Amy. The thought of a new adventure always excited Amy and got her full attention.

"There are many things to see and do here if one has the desire to seek them out," Kadluk advised the kids. He could see the change in their attitude with the mention of new adventures. It had gone from idle curiosity to anxious anticipation of what might lie ahead.

Ty remained skeptical; he was very suspicious of this old man. Gathering as much courage as he could, he decided to challenge Kadluk. *"Like what?"* Ty asked, *"What is there to see around here? It looks pretty barren to me."*

"Ty, don't be rude!" Amy said, scolding her brother.

"I'm not being rude; other than the mine and the dig, what is there to see? There's not even a tree within eyesight, only miles of unbroken tundra. I can't even

24

see the bay from here, it's so flat!" Ty shot back at his sister.

"I'm sure there are lots of things to do around here! You'll show us these things that you're talking about, won't you Kadluk?" inquired Amy. She had the sinking feeling that Ty's lack of enthusiasm might jeopardize any chance they may have to experience the adventures Kadluk was alluding to.

"I will help you. As I was taught, I will teach you and show you the secrets of the Inuit world. You must be inquisitive and seek knowledge on your own, and you must display your desire to explore and discover. Your enthusiasm will not go unnoticed by the deities," Kadluk told the kids, knowing that he now held their full attention. With the promise of sharing secrets, the full attention of his listeners could always be guaranteed. He noticed that even the defiant stance that Ty had taken had disappeared.

"What do the deities have to do with us?" Amy inquired, rather doubtfully.

"Sila was right, you are very sharp! The deities have everything to do with us, as they control our very being. Without their favor we would not exist, as you will see!" Kadluk said rather sternly, as if the

25

children should know this without being told.

*   *   *

"*How come you keep talking about deities?*" asked Amy in a questioning voice.

"*I am a Shaman!*" Kadluk proudly proclaimed.

"*What is a shaman?*" Asked Amy, "*I've never heard of a shaman.*"

"*We've never heard of a shaman either,*" piped in Ty and Parker.

The kids were awe-struck by what was happening. They were conversing with the Shaman and yet they were not speaking.

"*Only a shaman can communicate with the deities. I play an important role in the Inuit community; I ensure there is harmony with the people and the spirit world. Only a shaman can converse with the good and bad spirits that control our people's existence,*" said Kadluk.

"*How did you become a shaman?*" inquired Amy.

"*When I was young I displayed the qualities that my people desire in a shaman. My grandfather before me was a great shaman; under his guidance I learned the secret ways of the shaman. I was a good student and learned fast. I gained the respect of my people and I take pride in being able to help them in their times of need,"* said Kadluk with pride in his voice.

"What does a shaman do?" asked Amy.

"When an individual has exhausted his abilities to bring a desired result to a problem, he will seek me out and I will intervene with the deities on his behalf," replied Kadluk.

"What kind of problems would that be?" Amy inquired.

"The problems are many, and sometimes the answers are few. Even I, whom many consider to be one of the greatest shamans, have on occasion been out of favour with the deities. I may be called upon to heal the sick, to travel to the nether world to retrieve lost or stolen souls, or to set broken bones and bandage wounds. I have had to speak with the deities to improve the weather and to ensure that there are plenty of animals so that my people do not go hungry. My tasks are many and only the bravest shaman will succeed. Of all my skills, my ability to fly is the most important," Kadluk told the kids.

"You-can-fly?" exclaimed Amy, unsure that she had heard Kadluk correctly.

Ty and Parker were equally impressed by this revelation, and their imaginations were running rampant. They have never known anyone who could fly. Who is this old man, they wondered.

"Of course I can fly, how do you think I get to the moon to speak to the Tungat when there are no animals to hunt? How would I fly off to retrieve lost and stolen souls if I cannot fly?" Kadluk seemed rather disgusted.

"Who are the Tungat you go to the moon to talk to?" queried Ty.

"They are the spirits who control the supply of game animals and they live on the far side of the moon. If you wish to speak to them you must fly to the moon to have an audience. So you see, it is imperative that a shaman have the ability to fly," Kadluk proudly proclaimed.

"You have done this? You've actually flown to the moon?" cried Amy, doubting what she was hearing.

"Of course I have, I've been there many times. But there are times when a shaman must forgo his or her ability to fly and instead use conventional methods of travel, such as when they visit the all-powerful deities like Sedna and Sila. For there are times when only the gods can fly. Sedna is the sea goddess who rules over all the lesser spirits and monsters. She is the mother of both

28

land and sea creatures and therefore the provider of all life. Even the mightiest shamans have humbling limitations placed on their abilities, for the deities are all-powerful and a shaman is insignificant before them.

I have had to restore harmony between my people and the deities when they have sinned and lost favour. The laws must be observed so that the deities and the animals are shown the proper respect that will ensure a bountiful harvest for my people," Kadluk informed the kids, with an air of authority.

"It sounds like you have a lot to do," replied Amy.

*   *   *

"That's enough about me for now; in a few days you will be taking the mine safety course so that you will be able to operate the skidoos and the quads. Mind the instructor and learn how to operate the equipment so that you will be able to travel safely when you explore the countryside," said Kadluk.

"How do you know that?" asked Amy. *"No one has said anything to us about a course. Why would we be taking it?"*

"Munro will see that you take it, or you won't be able to operate the mine equipment," replied Kadluk.

"I hope you're right, I've always wanted to run one of those machines," piped in Ty.

"Do you use a skidoo?" asked Amy.

"No, I have no use for the new equipment, I travel the old ways as I have always done. I use my dog team in the winter and an umiak or a kayak in the summer," explained Kadluk.

"I know that a kayak is a one man boat used for hunting, but what's an umiak?" asked Amy.

"It's a large boat we use when we travel in the summer," answered Kadluk.

"We've never seen a real dog team," stated Amy.

"Maybe one day you will see my dog team, I always pass this way when I go to my trap line," stated Kadluk.

"We'd like that," Amy replied.

"Can we go with you and see your trap line?" Parker asked excitedly.

"Perhaps someday it will be possible,"Kadluk said to Parker.

The kids' imaginations were swimming with visions of the shaman flying to the moon to visit the deities. Could it be true? Could the old man really fly? From the attention being shown to him by the ladies in the kitchen, it was clear he was an important man in their community.

They remembered Mr. Munro telling them that this old man seemed to appear and disappear at will. Kadluk knew that Mr. Munro was going to put them in a safety course even though Mr. Munro couldn't speak to him. The kids were suddenly buoyed by the thought of all the excitement that would be coming their way, particularly the possibility of being able to operate the mine's equipment in the future.

"If you know so much, what else are we going to be doing that we don't know about?" asked Ty, rather smugly.

"Don't be rude Ty!" Amy scolded.

"I'm not being rude; if he knows so much, he can tell us what else is going to happen, can't he?" Ty said, looking at his sister.

"It is good to ask questions; to be inquisitive is to be knowledgeable. Only the gods are all knowing and with their charity they divulge some knowledge to me. I can also tell you that soon Munro will give you a tour of the mine. I don't know why Munro goes to all the trouble of mining these colourless diamonds when the coloured ones are much prettier," mused Kadluk.

"Coloured diamonds, I've never seen coloured diamonds," cried Amy.

"There are coloured diamonds but they're very rare," said Parker.

31

"*Leave it to you to know that,*" Amy said, smiling at her little brother.

"*Do you know where there are coloured diamonds, Kadluk?*" Ty inquired.

"*Perhaps, but that is for another time. Now go and see what Mr. Munro has to show you maybe he'll tell you why he digs for these.*"

Kadluk got up and walked to the door. "*I'm leaving now; I see that we will have many meetings in the time to come. Mark my words and learn what you can, for it will stand you in good stead when the time is right. You will have many adventures and you must be prepared.*"

Kadluk smiled and nodded his head to the kids as he passed their chairs, but spoke not a word. There was a twinkle in his eye that masked his age; the passing of time had not diminished his spirit.

As Kadluk neared them, Parker noticed there was something different about Kadluk's appearance. He couldn't contain his excitement any longer and blurted out, "*Jiminy-Willie-Peppers. What is that on your face? You've got more than wrinkles; what is that, Kadluk?*"

"*Parker, don't be so rude!*" scolded Amy, as she gave him a stern look.

Parker caught a glimpse of the tattoos that adorned Kadluk's face. From a distance they appeared to be age wrinkles and were not distinguishable, but there was no mistaking them up close. Just below his bottom lip ran a thin blue line from ear to ear. On his forehead above his eyes could be seen two blue tattoos resembling eyes.

"Parker is not being rude Amy, that is the inexhaustible innocence of youth speaking. Youth is always seeking answers. To question is not to be rude. How else does a person learn? They are tattoos Parker. It was a custom long ago that my people practiced, but is not prevalent in our society today. It is another custom that has been passed by time," Kadluk said as he continued walking.

"What are they for? What do they mean?" cried Parker.

"The line below my lip represents the water line, to show spirits that I need to have my head above water to live. If I happen to fall in the water the spirits will know how to help me. The two eyes on my forehead let all spirits know that I am always alert to danger and the malicious spirits will not be allowed to sneak up on me without being detected," Kadluk boasted proudly.

"How come they're blue?" inquired Ty.

"They're actually black but because they're

33

under my skin they appear blue," Kadluk advised the kids.

"How come the line below your lip is solid and the eyes appear to be made of dots?" questioned Ty.

"You're very observant to notice that! There are two ways to tattoo: one is with a needle and thread where the needle is passed just below the skin and then a substance soaked thread is pulled through the hole. The other is just using a needle to prick the skin and then rub the substance into the hole," Kadluk informed the kids.

"What do you mean by substance, and what did they put in the holes?" cried Amy.

"It is a mixture of lampblack, urine and graphite that is used in tattooing. Not only do the tattoos make a statement, they also protected us from evil spirits because lampblack, urine and graphite contain qualities that ward off evil spirits," Kadluk boasted.

"You're kidding, aren't you?" Ty asked. But he didn't need an answer, he could see that Kadluk wasn't kidding. This was something Kadluk had practiced all his life and believed in.

"Who gave you the tattoos?" Amy wanted to know.

"The elderly women are the tattoo artists, they are the ones who can sew the finest seams. They have learned the art as it was passed down through the

centuries," Kadluk informed the kids.

"*Wasn't it painful getting that needle run through your skin?"* Parker wanted to know.

"*Perhaps it was, but that was a long time ago, and doesn't matter anymore,"* Kadluk said as he went out the door.

After Kadluk left, the kids sat and thought about what had transpired. They didn't fully grasp what had just happened to them. Being able to converse with the Inua of other living and inanimate objects opened up a whole new world for them. This meeting would change them forever.

chapter iii

the revelation

Ty was the first to speak. *"What do you think of that?"* he cried, as he looked at Amy and Parker. *"Do you think that was a trick, talking to him that way, when Mr. Munro says he doesn't speak English and what are these Inuas anyway? I don't understand them! I'll just bet he talked to one of the mine workers and they told him what Mr. Munro was planning to do."*

"I don't think it's a trick because Kadluk is gone and we're still conversing through our Inuas. He's shown us a way, opened a door we didn't know existed until we met him. Also, Mr. Munro is the boss and he does what he wants to do, he doesn't tell anyone else what he's thinking. I get the same feeling that Mr.

37

Munro expressed, that there's more to this old man than meets the eye. There's something mysterious about him! I-like-him!" Amy declared.

"I think he's neat. This means we can talk to each other and no one will know we're even talking," Parker howled, as his eyes lit up.

"Well, we'll see tonight at supper, I'm going to ask Mr. Munro and then we'll see what's what!" declared Ty with as much authority as he could muster.

"Don't be too hasty with your criticism of the old man, you know very little about him," Amy scolded her brother.

"Yeah, take it easy on him, I've never seen anyone who could talk to us and not say a word. He not only talked to us, but he was on the other side of the room talking to the Inuit ladies at the same time. Now, if he didn't have special powers, how could he do this?" asked Parker with his eyes staring in wonder.

"We'll see tonight, when I ask Mr. Munro," blurted Ty.

"Be careful what you ask, you may not want to hear the answer," Parker warned, looking at his brother.

*   *   *

Because they were so preoccupied with the shaman, the kids didn't realize the rest of the afternoon had passed and their parents were coming in for supper. Their mother, Nadine, was first through the door and said, "There you are, I was wondering where you had gotten to."

"I'm sorry Mom I didn't realize it was so late, I meant to come back and see if you needed any more help, but we got tied up talking and the time just slipped by," Amy said, smiling at her mother.

"That's all right dear," Nadine said, "but remember we're new to this place and don't know all the dangers. Make sure you let me know where you are in the future," She gave Amy a quick pat on the shoulder.

"I will Mom," Amy replied.

The Munro's followed the Trapps into the kitchen where it was quite clear that Ty was anticipating their arrival.

"Mr. Munro," Ty said, as the Munros took their seats at the table, "Are you going to give us a safety course so we can drive the quads and skidoos?" he asked with a smirk on his face as he looked at Amy and Parker to observe their expressions.

39

"Why yes, funny you should bring that up, I was talking to our safety boss this afternoon and he is setting one up for you. For insurance purposes everyone has to take our safety course to operate our equipment. It's a good thing you mentioned it. When you're finished with the safety course I'll give you a tour of the mill and the pit, if everyone would like to see it?" Munro said, as he looked around the table at his quests.

From the expression that appeared on Ty's face, it was clear that this was not the answer he had been anticipating.

"Oh, we all want to see the mine," said Amy as she smiled at Ty.

"It will be awhile before I can set everything up, we're awful busy right now and can't spare the time," Mr. Munro told the group.

Ty didn't say a word out loud but he spoke to his sister through his Inua. *That doesn't prove anything.*

Amy replied, *"I think you've already answered your own question. We are communicating, yet not speaking; Kadluk has shown us a way we knew nothing about. It's true, a shaman has special powers. Do you think we have all these powers he speaks of?"*

"I-I don't know," Ty hesitantly responded.

40

Ty had a look on his face like he had just been kicked in the stomach. He had sassed Kadluk and now it looked like he probably had special powers. Had he insulted the old man, he wondered, would he bear a grudge and seek revenge? He comforted himself when he recalled that Kadluk said it was good to ask questions and be inquisitive. He assured himself that in the future he would show more respect for the things he did not understand.

*   *   *

"Dad, what is a shaman?" asked Amy.

"My, where did all this sudden interest come from? Is that what you were doing all afternoon, talking about the North?" asked Nadine, a questioning look on her face.

"Oh, a few things came up that we're just trying to find answers to," replied Amy as she displayed a weak smile on her face.

"A shaman is a priest of shamanism. That's a religion from northern Asia and it's based on good and evil spirits who can only be controlled or

41

influenced by a shaman. Some of the Eskimo, or Inuit, as most of them are known in Canada, still practice shamanism," Max replied.

"What is the difference between an Eskimo and an Inuit?" asked Amy.

"None, when the White man first came to North America they encountered the Algonquin Indians who told them about people living in the far North called the Eskimaux, meaning 'the eaters of raw flesh.' Thus the White man knew them as Eskimos. Some still call themselves Eskimos; however, most have reverted to their own name and call themselves Inuit or Yuiit meaning 'The People'," Max said to Amy.

"Kids," Gwen Munro sighed, "it's a joy to have them around, they're so inquisitive. Oh to be young again, and have their imaginations," she said with a laugh.

"Do you think we should tell them about Kadluk?" Parker asked Amy and Ty through his Inua.

"No!" replied Amy, *"I don't think they would understand. I can't believe it myself and it happened to me. I think we should just wait and see what happens next."*

When supper was finished the group left for their respective houses to get some sleep. Tomorrow would be another busy day!

chapter iv

walk in my mukluks

Sunday, September 22, 1985

Dear Diary,
 When I found myself alone on the tundra, I was really scared until Ty and Parker appeared.
 Amy

*   *   *

before Amy's head hit the pillow, she found herself alone on the tundra. She looked

45

around and at first could see no one. Then, far off to her left she could see two people walking towards her. She was startled and feared for her safety.

"Who are you?" she called to the approaching figures who were dressed in caribou parka, polar bear pants and sealskin mukluks, the same clothing Kadluk wore when she first met him. Looking down she was surprised to see that she too was wearing the traditional clothes of the Inuit.

"What are you yelling about, and why are we here?" came the reply from Ty's familiar voice.

Amy was relieved when she realized the two figures were her brothers, Ty and Parker.

"Jiminy-Willie-Peppers, I don't like this," Parker cried as he neared his sister.

"Do you think Kadluk has something to do with this?" asked Amy.

"Well if he does, why isn't he here?" demanded Ty.

"Where are we?" Parker asked while looking around.

"I don't know. We're somewhere on the tundra, but I'm not sure where - nothing looks familiar," Amy stated, as she searched for something she could relate to.

"Well I don't like it. If Kadluk has something to do with this then the next time I see him he'll have some explaining to do. I don't understand why we have to stand out here in the middle of nowhere. What's the sense in that? He better be ready to answer some questions," Ty said in his best authoritative voice.

"Well, get your questions ready because here he comes," Amy said to Ty as she observed the lone figure draw near.

Ty felt his confidence quickly fade as he saw the approaching figure and realized that it was indeed Kadluk. Ty was like the young buck that wanted to lead the herd but was unsure of what he was up against. He didn't know quite how to gauge this old man that possessed powers unknown to him.

It was because of this old man that the kids could communicate through their Inuas. Until they met Kadluk they didn't even know Inuas existed. What else did the old man have in store for them? What did he really want? Was he a friend or was he an enemy? Everything Kadluk had done so far appeared to have been done in

47

friendship; the kids had not been placed in danger - yet.

"Why are we here?" Amy asked through her Inua as Kadluk drew nearer.

"I figured you would have a few questions after you had time to think about what has happened," replied Kadluk.

"Ty has some questions he wants to ask you," Amy said as she nodded her head towards Ty.

"No-no that's okay, if you have any questions Amy you go ahead," Ty replied as his face reddened. Ty wasn't sure where he stood in the realm of things; Kadluk had him confused. He didn't want to invoke the wrath of a shaman because he didn't know the full extent of his powers.

"Why are we here and how did we get here?" asked Parker as he looked at Kadluk.

"That's a good question and after we've had our talk I'm sure things will be a lot clearer," Kadluk responded.

"We want to thank you for giving us the ability to talk to the Inuas," Amy said to Kadluk.

"Do not thank me, I gave you nothing. Had you not been born with the qualities of a shaman, you would not have been able to utilize that gift. I only showed you how to use it. It is the duty of the senior shaman to tutor and make an individual realize his full potential;

48

as my grandfather taught me, I will teach you," Kadluk told the kids.

"Do you mean we have the abilities of a shaman?" inquired Amy.

"No, you do not have the abilities of a shaman. You have the qualities that make a shaman, but only time will tell if you become a shaman," replied Kadluk.

"How do we do that?" asked Amy.

"You will be tested, for life itself is a test," answered Kadluk.

49

CHAPTER V

HE SHOWED ME THE WAY

"How did you become a shaman?" asked Parker.

'These young Kabloonas are so inquisitive, it has been a long time since anyone showed so much interest in the old ways,' Kadluk thought to himself.

"After I was born, I was adopted by my grandfather. He was a great shaman and I displayed the characteristics that could enable me to be a shaman, much like the characteristics that you Kabloonas seem to be displaying," said Kadluk with pride in his voice.

"Why would your grandfather adopt you? Did your parents die?" inquired Amy with a questioning look.

"No, it is a practice called Custom Adoption that is prevalent even today in our society. Usually, relatives of the child adopt the child. There could be many reasons for the adoption, but my grandmother and grandfather wanted me and so they adopted and raised me," Kadluk informed the kids.

"Were you born here?" asked Amy.

"Sit down I will tell you about myself and how I came to be here," said Kadluk as he gestured with his hand for the kids to sit.

The kids seated themselves on the ground in front of THE OLD ONE to listen to the story of his life.

"I was not born here, I was born on the Arctic Coast. After my grandparents adopted me, they ensured that I got to enjoy the things that every child enjoys while growing up. My grandfather taught me the way it was taught in the beginning," Kadluk said as the kids listened.

"Did you have any kids to play with Kadluk?" Amy asked.

"Of course I did, I played with the other kids in the village. We played games and explored new things just as any other child does," replied Kadluk.

"You did a lot of things with other kids, didn't you Kadluk?" Parker said enthusiastically as he

stared in admiration at Kadluk.

"My grandparents wanted me to have a normal childhood. When I grew older and was ready to take my place in the community, my grandfather would take me on hunts with him and make me observe the polar bear and the way it hunts the seal through the breathing holes in the ice," said Kadluk as he pointed at the ground to indicate that a hole would be at his feet.

"Why do they have breathing holes in the ice?" asked Ty.

"Seals can live under the ice but they have to have holes in the ice so that they can stick their noses out to get air," Kadluk told the kids.

"Oh I see," said Ty as he stared at Kadluk.

"From observing the polar bear I also learned respect for the pack ice and how to cross thin ice safely. In the beginning, the polar bear was the teacher and still, today, we learn from watching him," Kadluk paused to reflect.

"When I was ready, my grandfather taught me the secret chants so necessary to fulfill my duties as a shaman. I was the best hunter in my village; there was always meat in my pot. We always had more meat than we needed and my wife was honored to share with those the spirits did not favor. One day my cousin and I were hunting seals on the pack ice. Nanook the mighty polar

bear, snuck up on my cousin. I didn't know what was happening until I heard my cousin scream. When I turned around Nanook had his back to me, I ran at him and kicked him in the rear. This startled him and he dropped my cousin and spun around swinging his powerful forepaw at me. I ducked under his paw and punched him hard on the tip of his nose. Nanook was startled and he backed off a way and looked at me. He could see I was unarmed, but I stood my ground and this confused him. I stood over my cousin and protected him until Nanook left, and then took my cousin back to our village," explained Kadluk as the kids listened in wide-eyed wonderment.

The telling of the encounter with Nanook was one thing but the re-enactment of the attack by Kadluk held the kids spellbound. He played out how he attacked the bear and simulated ducking to evade the massive forepaw, then punching the air to emphasize the punch to the bear's snout. And last but not least, the aggressive stance he took while protecting his cousin from a further onslaught from the bear.

"Jiminy-Willie-Peppers, why didn't you talk to the bear's Inua? Why didn't you tell it to stop attacking your cousin?" Parker blurted out in his excitement.

"I tried to talk to the bear's Inua, I said, if you are hungry why don't you hunt your own seals? But it wouldn't reply," Kadluk said, shaking his head.

"Why wouldn't it talk to you?" Amy asked with concern in her voice.

"We can talk to the Inuas of animate and inanimate things, but they do not have to talk to us if they do not want to," Kadluk replied.

"Why wouldn't they talk to us?" Ty asked with concern in his voice.

"It could be for any number of reasons: maybe they have nothing to say to us, or maybe they just don't want to talk. I don't know why, that is just the way it is. We cannot control what others want to do, just as they cannot control what we want to do, nor why we want to do it," Kadluk informed the kids.

"Oh," responded Ty.

"After the encounter with the bear, my cousin sang my praises to all who would listen. My people looked to me for leadership and guidance. With my grandfather's teachings, my stature as a shaman grew and I became well respected by The People. As I grew older, life in the villages started to change. For some reason, many years ago the caribou stopped coming and a great famine hit the land. No one knew the reason for the disappearance of the caribou. The Tungat, the

55

spirits who control the supply of animals, would not hear our pleas to replenish the animals," said Kadluk.

"What did you eat if you had no caribou?" cried Amy with concern.

"The government stepped in and we had to move; they said they could take care of us better if we relocated. The people were starving - they had no choice but to move. Some maintained the conviction that we would return to our own lands when the caribou returned, but I knew this would never happen," Kadluk sighed and bowed his head.

"Where did they move you?" Ty wanted to know.

"My family and I were moved here to Rankin Inlet but others were moved to other locations. The nickel mine had just opened in Rankin Inlet and they needed workers. We were told that we could get jobs to support us during the famine so we wouldn't need the old ways to live. Our lives would never be the same again. The old ways quickly lost their appeal and for most would never return. Many of the old customs were abandoned as the people took jobs and no longer needed to depend on the land to sustain their way of life. Now the people had money and could purchase the food and clothing they needed from a store," said Kadluk.

"The first relocation took place in the 1930s and there were a few after that, but the last one was in the 1950s when the mine in Rankin was opened," Parker informed the group.

"How do you know that?" Amy inquired, looking at Parker.

"I read it at the library before we left Calgary," Parker told Amy with pride in his voice.

"Leave it to you to remember something like that," Amy said as she smiled at her brother and shook her head.

"My son and his family were also relocated here with me. I was not a young man when I arrived and the years since have taken their toll. I had difficulty adjusting to the Kabloonas' way of life, so I chose to continue with the old ways as much as I could. I could not have survived if the hunting and fishing had been taken from me, as these things make up the very life that I breathe. The freedom of the open trails is the only life that I could ever be true to. To be forced to take a routine job would have strangled me and left me an empty shell. I had to stay here to teach my grandson the old ways which his father too readily forgot. To see my grandson take to the old ways gave me a sense of happiness that I enjoyed," Kadluk proclaimed proudly.

"Where was your wife when all this was going on?" asked Ty.

"Ty don't get personal, that's none of your business," Amy said, giving him a stern look.

"It is good to be inquisitive and when you don't know something you should always ask. Life's journey is much easier if you have knowledge. When we relocated here my wife had already been in the tent of the never-ending feast in the nether world for many years," Kadluk shrugged his shoulders in despair.

"Where was she?" asked Ty, thinking he had not heard Kadluk correctly.

"It matters not; you will learn of the nether world and the never-ending feast at another time," Kadluk said, bringing the line of questioning to a close.

"How did the government bring you here?" queried Amy.

"I will tell you about the first time I saw the great metal bird. I had seen Kabloonas before but not very often and only briefly. When the famine hit, the Kabloonas came in the great metal bird. Until that time the Inuit believed that only a shaman could fly. I wondered if these Kabloonas, the ones they called the pilots, were shamans. Their people seemed to hold them in high regard. It wasn't long before I realized the pilots

58

were not shamans because they could not talk to their Inua, summon the spirits or heal the sick like a real shaman. They could not even talk to Sedna, the sea goddess who rules over all the lesser spirits and monsters; she is the mother of both sea and land animals and therefore the provider of all life. They pleaded ignorance for they didn't even know Sedna or any of the other deities that were necessary for the harmony of life. They talked only of a Supreme Being, but how could one being do all things necessary for harmony without the help of lesser deities? They were strange beings, these Kabloonas. They didn't know anything and yet they seemed to know a lot.

I talked to the pilots' Inua and they told me the pilots had been sent by their leaders to help us through the famine. I was the first to enter the great metal bird that swallowed things whole and spit them out unharmed. No one would enter the bird until the pilots took me for a short flight and we returned safely. I remember looking out those holes they called windows and seeing the earth far below. I had seen that before, being a shaman I had flown many times, but the experience would be something new to my people. Once we landed, The People reluctantly boarded the bird for relocation. That is how I came to be in this place at this time," Kadluk said as he shrugged his shoulders and looked at the ground.

CHAPTER VI

THE TREMBLING EARTH

"**W**hat does a shaman do?" asked Amy.

"He does many things that solicit fear and respect from his people. If the people do not fear and respect you, they will not follow you. A shaman can make the earth tremble with his footsteps, instilling fear in his people," Kadluk told the kids.

"This I've got to see!" Ty said as he looked at Amy and Parker with a smirk on his face.

"Ty don't be rude," Amy scolded.

"Do it Kadluk," cried Parker, "make the earth tremble!

Standing before them Kadluk said, *"be aggressive and be firm. Show your authority, for no other living thing has your abilities: you are the shaman. You and only you are the master of your domain. Only the deities have greater powers than you. When you demand respect, the earth trembles from your footsteps."* Then Kadluk took his stance, stomped his feet, and the earth trembled as if an earthquake had struck the land.

"Jiminy-Willie-Peppers," Parker howled, with eyes as big as saucers, *"I've never experienced anything like this."*

"Can I do that?" Amy shouted, as she jumped to her feet.

"We shall see," said Kadluk, *"do what I have shown you."*

Amy stood before the group and stomped her feet. Nothing happened.

"I can't do it, nothing happened," Amy sighed, rather dejectedly.

"Can a bird fly on its first try? Can an animal walk on its first try?" inquired Kadluk as he looked at Amy.

"No, they can't," Parker yelled excitedly.

"You mean our powers will grow as we grow and test them?" asked Amy.

62

"That is how it has always been and that is how it will always be. You learn as you grow and grow as you learn," Kadluk advised the kids as he spread his arms wide, as if he was embracing the world.

"Let me try again," Amy cried with excitement, as she stomped her feet.

"Not like that!" Kadluk said, as he stood before Amy, pulling himself to his full height he stiffened his arms, and stuck out his chest. *"Take this stance, stiffen your muscles and stamp your feet with authority. Use your mind - you're the shaman: believe in yourself. Everything trembles before you, for you are the shaman."*

Amy did what she was told and this time, the others could feel the ground tremble ever so slightly. Kadluk stood before the kids with his arms crossed on his chest, displaying the look of a proud father watching his kids realize their dreams.

"Jiminy-Willie-Peppers, you did it Amy!" Parker yelled with a big grin on his face.

"That is good, as you grow so will your powers," Kadluk said to Amy.

"Let me try," said Ty as he jumped to the fore.

He immediately took his aggressive stance and stomped his feet. Nothing happened.

63

"What am I doing wrong, why won't it work?" asked Ty looking desperately at Kadluk.

"You must concentrate, focus your mind, and direct your powers to what you want to do," Kadluk instructed Ty.

Ty focused on the task ahead and repeated the stomping.

"I can feel the earth shaking!" shouted Parker while he jumped up and down excitedly. Indeed he did feel the earth tremble. They all could.

Kadluk nodded his head and said to Parker, *"It's your turn to show us your power."*

Parker had benefited from watching Amy and Ty. He struck his pose and focusing his mind, he stomped his feet.

"You're doing it Parker," Amy cried with delight as her little brother stomped his feet and shook the earth.

Their new found powers delighted the kids and they stomped their feet and the earth trembled under them. Kadluk enjoyed watching the young Kabloonas, it reminded him of so long ago when he too did what they were doing as he was tutored by his grandfather. He wondered if his grandfather had felt the same satisfaction that he was now feeling.

CHAPTER VII

THE ELECTRICITY FLOWED

"*What else can a shaman do?*" Amy asked excitedly.

"*A shaman can make his body give off sparks,*" said Kadluk.

"*How can you do that?*" Ty asked with a frown on his face.

"*Watch,*" said Kadluk as he took his stance and concentrated. He stiffened his body, flung his arms outwards, and raised his hands to the heavens. Suddenly, sparks shot from his body and cracked like thunder!

"*Jiminy-Willie-Peppers!*" shouted Parker, as his eyes grew large as saucers.

Amy and Ty stood staring at Kadluk. They had never seen anything like the display before them. The sparks that sprang from his body startled them and they recoiled, worried that they were going to get an electric shock from him.

"*Are you alright?*" Amy asked Kadluk with concern in her voice.

"*I'm fine,*" Kadluk replied, and gave a satisfied grunt.

"*Are we supposed to be able to do that?*" inquired Ty, with a look of astonishment on his face, as if he didn't believe what he was seeing.

"*Of course, any shaman can give off sparks from his body,*" Kadluk told the kids as his chest swelled with pride.

"*Let me try,*" cried Parker as he stood before the group, pushed out his chest, and took his stance. Parker quickly flung his arms wide and raised his hands to the heavens. Nothing happened.

"*What's wrong, where are the sparks?*" he asked, looking dejectedly at Kadluk.

"*You're not using your mind, remember: you*

68

are the shaman," Kadluk said, *"Concentrate, believe in what you are doing, and try again."*

Again Parker took his stance and, concentrating with all his might, flung his arms wide and raised his hands to the heavens. The sparks danced across his body and flew from his fingertips, clapping like thunder.

"Did you see that?" Parker said to Amy and Ty with an enormous grin on his face. *"I never thought I would ever be able to do anything like this. It's like magic."*

"My turn," cried Ty as he took his stance and concentrated with all his might for he too felt the power. *"I-am-the-shaman,"* he cried as he flung his arms wide and raised his hands to the heavens. Quickly the sparks danced across his body and raced to his fingertips to be shot into space while crashing like thunder.

"None of my friends will ever believe this," Ty said to no one in particular as he looked with disbelief at his hands.

"Let me try that," said Amy as she took her stance. Concentrating with all her might she flung her arms wide and reached for the heavens. The sparks raced across her body and shot up her arms only to be flung into space like a million stars.

"There," Amy said, *"I knew I could do it if you guys could."*

"You are all learning very quickly," Kadluk advised the kids.

chapter viii

teach us to fly

"You told us before that you could fly. Can all shamans fly?" Amy inquired.

"Of course all shamans can fly, it is the greatest power that a shaman has. His ability to fly is very important, because without this skill he could not perform the tasks required of him," Kadluk proudly told the kids.

"Then, let's see you fly!" demanded Ty.

"Ty," Amy said giving her brother a stern look.

"*Well he said he could fly; let's see him do* it!" Ty retorted.

"*Kadluk, who is that?*" Amy cried, pointing to the lone figure approaching them.

"*That is my assistant, he's coming to help us prepare,*" Kadluk said as he looked towards the man.

"*Prepare for what?*" Ty asked, with a quick glance at the assistant.

"*Jiminy-Willie-Peppers, he's going to help us prepare for flying! Isn't he Kadluk?*" Parker shouted.

"*Yes Parker, that is what he is going to do. Flying is something that is not taken lightly. I only fly after I have determined that that is the best course of action to take. On some occasions before flying, a shaman must be bound tightly, because if you move, your Inua, spiritual occupant or spirit helper, will not be able to locate you when it returns and it will be lost forever,*" Kadluk advised his listeners.

"*Then it's not you that flies, it's your Inua,*" said Ty rather proudly.

"*That is correct, when I send my Inua on a journey it is me and I am it, for only a shaman has the ability to communicate with his Inua and send it on journeys. Despite this, I can also fly if the situation warrants it and then I do not need to be bound!*" Kadluk stated with authority.

"Oh!" Ty found himself saying as he stared at Kadluk.

"What is he carrying?" Amy asked Kadluk as she looked at the object the assistant had in his left hand.

"That is the drum that we will use," Kadluk proudly proclaimed.

"Use - use for what? What does a drum have to do with flying?" cried Amy.

"The drum is necessary for flight; without the drum, flight cannot be achieved, as you will see!" Kadluk stated.

As the assistant drew closer the drum could be seen more clearly. Parker never took his eyes from the assistant or the drum. It fascinated him and he could see that it was made of skin stretched over a wooden frame. From the drum hung strips of hide with feathers attached to the ends of the strips. The handle of the drum resembled a bird and was firmly held in the assistant's left hand.

"Kadluk is that a carving of a bird attached to the drum?" Parker inquired peering closely at the drum.

"Yes it is! We are going to fly, and only the deities and the birds are able to fly through the air. Therefore it is necessary to appease the birds, so they will welcome us into their realm as guests and not as

75

intruders. The handle shows the birds that we respect their domain. The feathers attached to the drum show the birds we mean them no harm. We will only use their space to fly in; we will not disturb it, and we will leave it as we found it. The feathers also symbolize the transition we will make from the land to the air and back again, because without feathers birds cannot fly," Kadluk informed the kids.

"Did you make the drum Kadluk?" Amy wanted to know as she watched the feathers attached to the drum flutter in the breeze.

"Of course I made the drum!" Kadluk said rather indignantly.

The assistant sat down when he reached the group. Kadluk gestured to the drummer and the Boom-Boom-Boom of the drum filled the air.

"Come sit in a circle with the drummer," Kadluk said to the kids as he pointed to the ground beside his assistant.

The kids quickly did what they were told and sat where Kadluk indicated they should. The drum continued its steady beat, Boom-Boom-Boom.

"AIIIEEE," Kadluk began to chant as he took his place in the circle and the drum continued to beat, Boom-Boom-Boom.

On and on the drumbeat continued with Kadluk singing the secret chants of the shaman. He was summoning the spirits to assist him on his quest to fly. The steady beat of the drum and Kadluk's chanting produced a euphoric state. The kids joined Kadluk and sung the secret chants of the shaman. They chanted, "AIIIEEE," in unison as the drumbeat continued, Boom-Boom-Boom.

"The way is clear, follow me," Kadluk cried.

The kids could feel themselves pass through the drum as they followed THE OLD ONE into the heavens.

"Jiminy-Willie-Peppers!" Parker shouted as he flew through the air. *"Look what I can do,"* he cried.

"Where are we going to go?" Amy excitedly asked as she looked at Kadluk.

"Where would you like to go?" Kadluk inquired.

"I don't know I've never flown before. Where do you usually go?" Amy asked, as she floated in the air.

"Usually the task I'm performing determines where I go when I fly, but because I'm showing you your capabilities, we can do whatever you like," Kadluk said matter of factly.

"Let's fly up to the clouds," Parker shouted.

"Yeah, let's fly to the clouds! Come on Parker I'll race you," Ty said as he flew towards the low hanging clouds, with Parker close on his heels.

"We better catch up to them, heaven only knows what they'll get into if we're not with them," Amy exclaimed to Kadluk, as she took off to follow her brothers.

When Amy and Kadluk reached the clouds, Parker and Ty were already walking on them.

"Look at me Amy, look how I can bounce on the clouds. They're really spongy," cried Parker as he jumped up and down on the heavily laden rain cloud.

"Come on you two, we've got a lot to do yet," Amy reminded her brothers.

"Ah, do we have to go already? This is fun," Parker sighed.

"Yes, we have to go, I have other things I must show you before I leave," Kadluk informed the kids.

Reluctantly the boys followed Kadluk and found themselves again seated in the circle with The Old One's assistant. Boom-Boom-Boom went the drum as the steady rhythm continued.

"What are we going to do now?" Amy asked as she looked searchingly at Kadluk.

"We are going to send our Inuas out of our bodies to enjoy the thrill of flying," Kadluk informed the kids.

"How are we going to do that?" Amy cried.

"First we must be bound, we cannot send our Inuas out to fly without being bound," Kadluk advised the kids.

"How can you bind yourself?" Ty wanted to know.

"I cannot bind myself; my assistant binds me. It is important that one does not move while your Inua is away or your Inua will not be able to find you when it returns. That is why we are bound tightly while laying on the ground. You are fortunate as you are together, using slipknots you will be able to tie one another and you can act as your own assistants. I will show you how to do this. However if you do not have an assistant one of you will have to stay behind to beat the drum." Kadluk informed the kids.

"Why?" asked Ty looking dumbfounded.

"Listen to the drum - without its beat, flight cannot be taken!" Kadluk said, as his assistant beat the drum and chanted. Boom-Boom-Boom went the drum. Kadluk continued with his instructions as he began to chant and the kids joined in. *"AIIIEEE,"* they chanted as they called upon the

spirits to assist them on their quest for flight.

"What do you get bound with?" asked Amy.

"Check your pockets, a shaman always carries strips of sealskin to use as bindings," replied Kadluk.

Upon checking their pockets the kids found this to be true, for each had several lengths of sealskin strips.

"Show us how our Inuas fly Kadluk," Parker shouted with excitement.

Even though he was chanting, Ty was a little hesitant as he sat and watched what was happening with interest.

"First I must show you how to tie yourselves so that you do not move while your Inua is on a mission," Kadluk said to the kids.

"Where do we start?" cried Amy.

"Start with me Kadluk!" Parker blurted out in his excitement.

"Now lay on the ground and start with the legs, they're to be tied tightly so that we cannot walk away. Bind them tight enough to restrict mobility, but not so tight that it cuts off blood circulation. Then the arms are bound to the torso, this is done with slip knots because when your Inua returns the slip knots are easily loosened even though you are bound tightly," Kadluk said as he tied Parker with the sealskin strips.

"*That looks easy enough,*" commented Ty as he observed the scene being played out before him.

"*Good I'm glad it does. Now you can bind me, but first I will bind my legs and then you can bind my arms,*" Kadluk advised Ty.

"*I'll help you Ty,*" Amy said.

Kadluk and Parker were soon bound and they watched as Amy and Ty first bound their legs and then used the slipknots to secure their arms to their torsos. The assistant never missed a beat and the drum continued its steady Boom-Boom-Boom as the group chanted.

"*What do we do now?*" Amy inquired, as she lay on the ground.

"*What would you like to do?*" Kadluk asked.

"*I want to fly,*" yelled Parker.

"*Then fly we shall, the way is open, follow me,*" said Kadluk.

As they watched, Kadluk's Inua emerged from his torso and hung suspended in air just above his prostate body.

"*Jiminy-Willie-Peppers, do you see that!*" exclaimed Parker.

Amy and Ty laid where they were tied and tried to comprehend what they were seeing. Never

81

before had they seen an apparition appear before them.

"*Is it a ghost?*" cried Amy.

"*No, it is me, Kadluk,*" said Kadluk.

"*You look like a ghost!*" exclaimed Amy.

"*It's my Inua, come join me and we shall fly,*" Kadluk said to the kids.

"*How do we do that?*" questioned Amy.

"*Remember you-are-the-shaman! Send your Inua out of your body so that you may experience the thrill of flying,*" Kadluk stated.

"*Wait for me Kadluk, I'm coming,*" shouted Parker.

The kids concentrated and soon their Inuas were suspended in space above their bodies.

"*Kadluk was right, it-is-me and I-am-it,*" exclaimed Amy.

"*Jiminy-Willie-Peppers! This is spooky looking down at your own body,*" Parker said.

"*Well, are you ready to fly?*" asked Kadluk.

Ty was dumbfounded. He didn't know what to say, he was again doing something he thought was impossible.

"*Look at me,*" Parker shouted as he somersaulted through the air.

82

"That's nothing watch this," Ty said as he spiraled like a corkscrew.

"You boys stop that and come here while we try to figure out what we're going to do," said Amy to her brothers.

"Let them have some fun. I remember the first time I flew and what an exhilarating feeling it was. I can still recall the satisfied look on my grandfather's face, it was like he realized for the first time that I would one day be a shaman like him," said Kadluk to Amy.

"I suppose you're right, they can't do any harm and they seem to be enjoying themselves tremendously," Amy replied.

"They will have to come back soon, as I still have to explain one more thing that a shaman has to do for his people," said Kadluk.

"What is that?" asked Amy.

"A shaman is the healer of his people; he must administer the medicine needed to heal. Sewing up cuts and amputating damaged parts of the body are all tasks that a shaman must see to. A shaman's duties are many and he must be strong to face all his responsibilities for his people rely on his abilities," said Kadluk.

"Oh, we're familiar with medical procedures

because we've all had first aid and CPR training," Amy advised Kadluk.

"This is good, for you may be called upon to administer to the sick; one must be ready to help his people at all times," Kadluk told her.

"Should I call Ty and Parker back?" Amy asked.

"Yes, call them, it is time to go," replied Kadluk.

When Amy called to Ty and Parkers' Inuas they stopped skylarking and returned to their bodies.

"Turn towards me," Kadluk said to Ty. *"I will show you how to loosen the slip knots to free yourself."*

Once Ty was freed he untied the rest.

"What are we going to do now?" Amy asked Kadluk.

"It is time to go - we have done enough for today. You now know what a shaman is capable of doing and what is expected of him or her," replied Kadluk.

"But I don't want to go yet, I want to fly some more," Parker cried.

"You'll have lots of chances to fly in the future;

your adventures are just beginning," Kadluk said.

"But you haven't told us how we got here in the first place, I just remember laying down," Amy pleaded.

"I summoned you!" Kadluk declared.

"Jiminy-Willie-Peppers, how did you do that?" queried Parker.

"It matters not, there are some things you will never understand," Kadluk told the kids as he turned to go.

"But-but, don't go! I have more questions!" Amy yelled to Kadluk as he disappeared into the vast expanse of the tundra.

"I knew it - there's more to The Old One than we'll ever know. He can do things we'll never be able to do or understand!" Parker stated as Kadluk vanished from sight.

The last thing Amy heard as her head hit the pillow, was her brother Ty agreeing with Parker while they stood alone on the Tundra.

* the end *

GLOSSARY

Inua – (inh'oo ah) n, the spiritual occupants, or spirit helpers, that reside in all living or inanimate things

Inuit – The People

Inuktitut – n, the language of the Inuit

Komatik - (koh-ma-tik) n, a sled with wooden runners and crossbars bound with animal hides

Mukluk – an Inuit skin boot

Nanook – polar bear

Sedna – a sea goddess who ruled over all the lesser spirits and monsters. She was considered to be the mother of both land and sea creatures and therefore the provider of all life

Shaman – (Sham-man n, 1. a priest of shamanism. 2. a medicine man or witch doctor of a similar religion. (they were thought to have special abilities in relating to the supernatural powers)

Shamanism – (sham-man-iz-zum) n, a religion of northern Asia, based on a belief in good and evil spirits who can be influenced or controlled only by the shamans

Sila – an all-pervasive spirit which resides in the air

Tarrak – a dark, angry, enraged and malicious spirit. If relatives did not adhere to certain taboos after a person's death the dead person's soul became enraged and malicious. This dark angry spirit was known to some Inuit as a personal shade or tarrak.

Tundra - n, a vast treeless Arctic region with permanently frozen subsoil

Tungak - (see tungat)

Tungat - (plural of tungak) the spirits who controlled the supply of game animals

The Author

Lawrence was born and raised in Alberta. 37 years of his adult life was spent serving in the Canadian Armed Forces and the Royal Canadian Mounted Police. The author draws on 10 years of living in the Yukon and the Northwest Territories for the inspiration for his stories. Retirement finds him again in Alberta where he presently lives with his wife Judith. They have 2 children and 6 grandchildren.

The Illustrator

Rob Adams, son of Lawrence Adams; when he is not working on his fathers illustrations, can be found working on game designs. Trained in Visual Communication, Rob currently works in the field of video games, juggling roles of a producer and game designer. Rob has had first hand experience of living and visiting many of the places described in the Trapps Family Adventure books.

Watch for future books by Lawrence Adams as the Trapps Family Adventures continue to explore the mysteries of the north.

The Amulet
The Creator
The Stolen Soul
The Mine
The Famine
Who Walks on my Land
Who Swims in my Waters
Who Flies in my Skies
The Spirit of Marble Island
The Search for the Red Diamond
The Little People
The Rescue

Join Amy, Ty and Parker as they continue to seek answers to life's adventures on the frozen tundra.

GIVE A "**LAWRENCE E.R. ADAMS**" BOOK TO A FRIEND

Trapps Publishing
P.O. Box 212
Irricana, AB T0M 1B0

Send to:
Name:_____
Street:_____
City:_____
Province/   Postal/
State:_____Zip Code_____
Please Send:
"THE OLD ONE"   _____ X @ $9.95 =_____

Shipping and handling for first book @ $4.00
plus $1.00 each additional Book   =_____
                                        6% GST =_____
                        Total amount enclosed: _____

Make cheque or money order payable to:
TRAPPS PUBLISHING
Price subject to change without prior notice.
ORDERS OUTSIDE OF CANADA must be paid in U.S.
funds by cheque or money order drawn on U.S. or Canadian
Bank.
Sorry no C.O.D.'s.

GIVE A "**LAWRENCE E.R. ADAMS**" BOOK TO A FRIEND

Trapps Publishing
P.O. Box 212
Irricana, AB T0M 1B0

Send to:
Name:_____
Street:_____
City:_____
Province/   Postal/
State:_____Zip Code_____
Please Send:
"THE OLD ONE"   ____ X @ $9.95 =_____

Shipping and handling for first book @ $4.00
plus $1.00 each additional Book   =_____
                                      6% GST =_____
                    Total amount enclosed: _____

Make cheque or money order payable to:
TRAPPS PUBLISHING
Price subject to change without prior notice.
ORDERS OUTSIDE OF CANADA must be paid in U.S.
funds by cheque or money order drawn on U.S. or Canadian
Bank.
Sorry no C.O.D.'s.